D1008283

YOU CHOOSE
BOOKS

CINDERELLA

AN INTERACTIVE FAIRY TALE ADVENTURE

by Jessica Gunderson

illustrated by
Ayesha Rubio

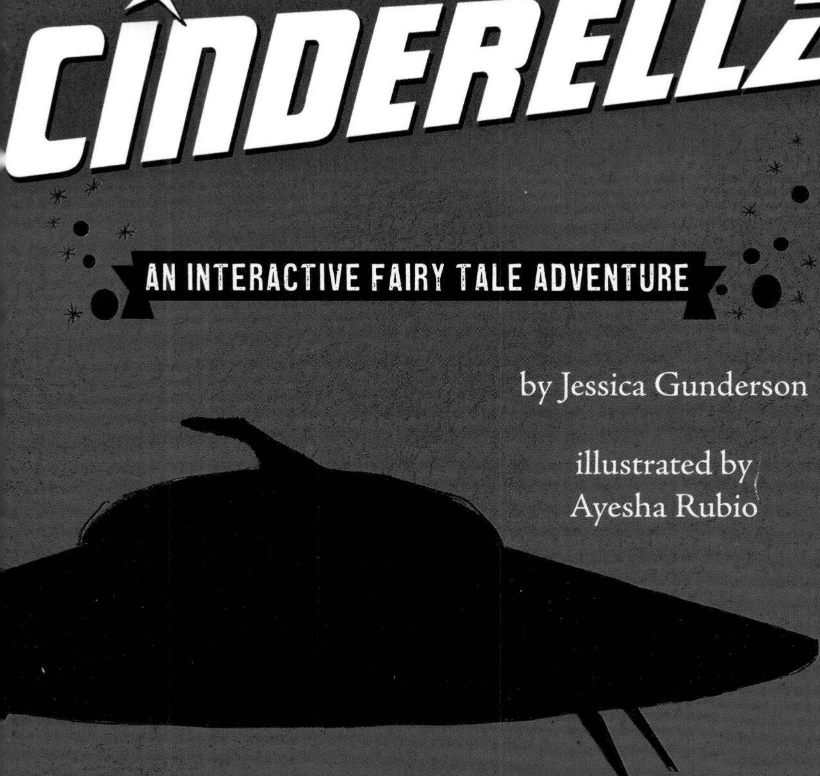

CAPSTONE PRESS
a capstone imprint

You Choose Books are published by Capstone Press,
1710 Roe Crest Drive, North Mankato, Minnesota 56003
www.capstonepub.com

Library of Congress Cataloging-in-Publication Data
Gunderson, Jessica, author.
  Cinderella : an interactive fairy tale adventure / by Jessica Gunderson.
    pages cm. — (You choose: fractured fairy tales)
  Summary: In this You Choose adventure, Cinderella can be a modern-day girl living
in a city, a young man in a medieval fairy tale, or a girl in a futuristic space society—
the choice is up to the reader.
  ISBN 978-1-4914-5854-9 (library binding)
  ISBN 978-1-4914-5927-0 (paperback)
  ISBN 978-1-4914-5939-3 (eBook PDF)
1. Plot-your-own stories. [1. Fairy tales. 2. Plot-your-own stories.] I. Title.
  PZ8.B6732Ci 2015
  [Fic]—dc23   2015006285

Editorial Credits
Kristen Mohn, editor; Ted Williams, designer; Nathan Gassman, creative director;
Tori Abraham, production specialist

Image Credits
Shutterstock: solarbird, background

Printed in Canada.
032015   008825FRF15

TABLE OF CONTENTS

ABOUT YOUR ADVENTURE

You're exhausted. You're always being worked to the bone and you're treated cruelly. You see no glimmer of hope until one day a chance for escape comes in the form of an invitation. But getting yourself to the big event is just the beginning of your adventure.

In this fairy tale, you control your fate. Brush the ashes off yourself and take charge! You make choices to determine what happens next ... with a little help from your fairy godparent.

Chapter One sets the scene. Then you choose which path to read. Follow the directions at the bottom of the page as you read the stories. The decisions you make will change your outcome. After you finish one path, go back and read the others for new perspectives and more adventures.

A CHANCE TO ESCAPE

You are tired after a long day of work. When you open the door to your home, ready to rest your aching body, you are greeted by your two step-siblings. It's not a friendly greeting.

"Polish my shoes!" one of them shouts.

"Mend my socks!" the other commands. "And make me some supper. I'm starving!"

"And take out that trash! It smells worse than you do!"

You sigh. Life with them isn't easy, now that your father is gone.

7

Many years ago, after your mother died, your father married a woman with two children. At first you were happy to have playmates. The children weren't very nice to you, but your father made things bearable.

But over the years, you learned just how mean and rotten your step-siblings were. And they got meaner as they grew older. They ordered you around, stole your things, and blamed you when they did something wrong. Then your father died too, and you became nothing more than a servant in your own home. Your stepmother was no help

at all.

Now you go to the kitchen to make dinner. As you cook, you dream about a different life. A life without your wicked family. A life where you are appreciated and loved. Maybe someday you'll have a chance to escape.

TO BE A MODERN-DAY GIRL LIVING IN A CITY,
TURN TO PAGE II.

TO BE A YOUNG MAN IN A MEDIEVAL FAIRY TALE,
TURN TO PAGE 47.

TO BE A GIRL IN A FUTURISTIC SPACE SOCIETY,
TURN TO PAGE 77.

CHAPTER 2

A PUMPKIN, A SHOE, AND A SCHOOL DANCE TOO

"Hurry up!" your stepsister Anabel hollers over the blaring TV. "I'm starving!"

You glance at Anabel sprawled out on the couch watching a dumb "reality" show about encounters with fairies. She hasn't moved since you left for work eight hours ago.

Her twin, Diane, is on the chair, furiously texting her friends. "Yeah," she says without looking up. "We've been waiting forever!"

You're tired. The last thing you want to do is cook. You've been cooking all day at the Pizza Palace. But you know if you refuse, your stepsisters will tell your stepmother, and you'll get grounded. So you make your stepsisters dinner. They don't even say thank you.

"You're welcome," you mutter.

"What was that, Cinderella?" Anabel taunts. You cringe. You hate your nickname. Anabel and Diane have been calling you that since you started at the Pizza Palace because you come home covered in cinders from the wood-burning pizza oven. And now they've got the whole school calling you that awful name.

"Nothing," you answer sweetly. You fill the sink to start the dishes. You overhear your sisters talking about the school dance, the Harvest Ball, this weekend.

Anabel is wondering which shoes to wear from her wall-to-wall shoe collection. She's got every style and color imaginable.

When you are finished with your chores, you walk to the bank to deposit your paycheck. You realize you've finally reached your goal—enough money to buy a car! You go straight to the used car lot. The only car you can afford is a bright, hideous orange, but you really need a car so you won't have to walk all the way to work anymore. Plus, if you had a car, you could go to the Fashion Design conference in New York. You've heard that your favorite designer, Vivian Marshall, might be there.

13

But the conference is still a month away. Maybe a better car will come along in the meantime.

TO BUY THE CAR, TURN TO PAGE 14.

TO WAIT FOR ANOTHER CAR, TURN TO PAGE 17.

You buy the car and feel proud driving it home. It may be orange, but you earned this car all by yourself. You decide to affectionately name it Rusty.

You pull in the driveway and see your stepsisters gawking out the window. When you go inside, you hear shrieks of laughter. "What's that you brought home?" Anabel says. "It looks like a big rusty pumpkin!"

Diane doubles over with laughter. "Cinderella drives … a pumpkin!" she gasps.

You seethe with anger but know there's no point in arguing. They'd never understand what it feels like to earn something through hard work. To get them off your back, you change the subject. "So, have you decided what you're wearing to the dance?" you ask.

They forget about the car and rush into their bedrooms, coming back with armloads of dresses to try on.

"What are *you* wearing?" Diane asks, turning away from admiring her reflection.

"I'm not going," you admit. "I used all my money to buy the car."

TURN THE PAGE.

15

Diane pauses and bites her lip, clearly scheming. "Well, how about if I buy you any dress you want, and in return, I get to drive your car to the dance? I mean, even though it's hideous, it's still a car," she snorts.

You think it over. Your stepmother has told the twins that they can't have a car until next year, when she cashes in the rest of your father's inheritance. Naturally, she's never offered you a car at all.

You could drive yourself to the dance in Rusty, but then you'd have to sew your own dress. Between school and work, you don't think you'll have time. And you wouldn't mind walking to the dance, if it meant you could wear something beautiful. There's a Vivian Marshall dress you've had your eye on.

TO ACCEPT DIANE'S OFFER, TURN TO PAGE 19.

TO SEW YOUR OWN DRESS, TURN TO PAGE 20.

"Hmm," you say to the car salesman. "I think I'll pass." It's bad enough that the kids call you Cinderella. You don't need to encourage them by driving a pumpkin around.

The next day as you are walking to school, you are shocked to see the bright orange car coming down the street. Inside is Diane. When she pulls into the parking lot, a bunch of other kids rush toward her. "I love it!" Diane's friend Bridget squeals. "Orange is the coolest!"

It figures. All day long all anyone can talk about is Diane's orange car. Oh well, you think. At least now you have money to buy yourself a decent dress. Maybe not the designer dress you've always wanted, but still, a nice one.

TURN THE PAGE.

A few days later, as you are getting ready to go shopping, Diane bursts into your room. "I'm sick of my car," she says. "It's so annoying. I didn't know I had to buy gas for it! Do you want it? I'll sell it to you for a good price."

If you buy the car, you won't have enough money for a dress. But having that car would make your life so much easier.

TO BUY A DRESS INSTEAD, TURN TO PAGE 25.

TO BUY THE CAR FROM DIANE, TURN TO PAGE 37.

You search online until you find the perfect dress. Diane whips out her credit card and punches in the numbers. "There!" she says. "Now you'll have a dress to wear, and I'll have a car to drive to the dance."

On the day of the dance, just in time, your dress arrives. You rip open the box eagerly, but what you pull out is the ugliest brown dress you've ever seen. And it's the wrong size. You throw it back into the box. Diane is watching with fake pity in her eyes. "Isn't that the dress you wanted?" she asks. "Too bad. They must have made a mistake. But ... we had a deal." She smiles sweetly. "Hand over your car keys, please."

19

You wonder if Diane purposely messed up your order. You wouldn't put it past her.

TO REFUSE, TURN TO PAGE 21.

TO HAND OVER THE KEYS, TURN TO PAGE 23.

You tell Diane no and she storms off. You bought that car fair and square, and you'll be driving it to the dance.

You find some vintage fabric in the attic and get to work sewing your dress. Maybe someday you'll be a famous designer just like your idol, Vivian Marshall. Even though you can't spend as much time on the dress as you would like, when you are finished with it, you are pleased. But the dress still needs some lace and maybe a few sparkles. On the day of the dance, you go to the mall to see what you can find.

20

In the middle of the mall you see an old woman selling sewing supplies from a vendor stall you've never noticed before. Exactly what you need!

TURN TO PAGE 28.

"Sorry," you tell Diane. "The deal was that you'd buy me a dress to wear to the dance. And I wouldn't be caught dead in this dress. The deal is off."

Diane's eyes blaze with anger. "Fine!" she says. "I didn't want to take your ugly car anyway. I wouldn't be caught dead in that!"

You watch her stomp from the room, and then you go to your closet and stare at your pitiful collection of clothes. You have only one dress, which is old and barely fits you anymore. You put it on anyway, having no other choice.

21

At least you have your car. You hop in and head for the Harvest Ball. You're almost there when you hear a weird sound in Rusty's engine. *Chug-chug-grr. Chug-chug-grr.* Uh-oh. You don't know much about cars, but you know this can't be good. You pull over.

TURN THE PAGE.

When you get out of the car, you see an old woman standing on the sidewalk. She waves at you. You glance around and see a handsome boy on the other side of the street. He's waving too.

TO TALK TO THE OLD WOMAN, TURN TO PAGE 28.

TO TALK TO THE HANDSOME BOY, TURN TO PAGE 34.

22

You let out a heavy sigh. Diane taps her foot impatiently, hand outstretched. Although you highly doubt it, maybe it really was a shipping mistake. There's no way to know for sure.

You sigh again. "A deal's a deal," you say and drop the keys into her hand. She squeals with delight and rushes away.

You go to your closet and put on your best dress—your only dress—which is out-of-style but not yet old enough to be vintage. You're no longer sure you even want to go to the dance. This dress will only give the kids more to make fun of.

TURN THE PAGE.

You head out for the dance on foot. After a few blocks, you pass a pumpkin patch on quiet street. Out of the corner of your eye, you think you see an old woman in the pumpkin patch. She seems to be waving at you. What could she want?

You're about to go talk to her when Anabel, Diane, and their friends go screeching by in your orange car. One of them launches a rotten pumpkin out the window, which smashes all over your dress. You've finally had enough and you begin to cry.

24 Forgetting all about the old woman, you turn and walk home, never knowing you've just missed meeting your fairy godmother.

THE END

TO FOLLOW ANOTHER PATH, TURN TO PAGE 9.

You tell Diane that you don't want the car. You've learned not to trust her. You assume she's probably ruined the car somehow and that's why she really wants to get rid of it. Instead you walk to the mall and use some of your savings to buy the prettiest dress you can find. You can't wait until the dance! Finally you might be noticed—as a beautiful girl, not plain, grungy Cinderella. As you are heading out of the mall, you keep peering at the dress in the bag. It's so lovely, with sparkles and satin and flowing lace.

As you weave through the parking lot, you hear tires squeal and an engine roar. A bright orange car is barreling straight for you!

25

TURN THE PAGE.

You jump out of the way, hitting your elbow on the bumper of a large SUV. Plop! You drop your shopping bag, and the dress falls out. Right into an oily puddle.

You snatch up the dress, but it's too late. It's soaked and grimy. Then you hear cackling. You look up to see Diane and Anabel leaning out the orange car's windows. "Drop something?" Diane calls. They cackle again and roar away.

You watch the taillights disappear. Apparently the car still works after all. You sigh and look down at the dress again, hoping you can save it.

Suddenly you remember an episode of *Real Livin' with Vivian*—Vivian Marshall's TV show in which she tackles real-life fashion disasters. Wasn't there one about turning spills and stains into "beauty spots"? You better go home right away to watch it.

"Hey!" calls a girl's voice.

You look up to see a girl dressed in a bright blue shirt and cut-off jeans. If you're not mistaken, the shirt is from Vivian Marshall's ready-to-wear line. "I think I can help you with that," the girl says, looking down at the dress. "Follow me!"

TO FOLLOW THE GIRL IN BLUE, TURN TO PAGE 32.

TO GO HOME AND WATCH REAL LIVIN' WITH VIVIAN, TURN TO PAGE 44.

The old woman cackles as you approach her. She eyes you up and down. "I have what you need," she croaks. You think talking to her might be a mistake. She reaches into a strange trunk. You are surprised when she pulls out a gorgeous, glimmering dress.

"A Vivian Marshall?" you sputter.

The old woman nods excitedly. "It's made of high-tech fabric with tiny electrical charges inside. When you move, it lights up." She shakes the skirt and it twinkles with bright, popping colors.

"That's incredible!" you exclaim.

"You'll be the belle of the ball," the woman says.

"How much?" you ask hesitantly. You are sure you won't be able to afford it.

"You can rent it," she says. "It's a slow night, so I'll drop my price to ten dollars!" You can't believe your luck. "But you need to give it back to me by midnight," the old woman warns. "After five hours, the tiny wires inside start to fry. The dress needs to be put immediately into this special solar-panel box to recharge, or it will be ruined."

You pay her and agree to meet her at midnight **29** outside the school. "Not a minute late!" she says.

You rush home to get ready. Once the dress is on, you realize what you're missing—shoes.

TURN THE PAGE.

You knock on Anabel's bedroom door, but there's no answer. She must've already left for the dance. Her shoe closet door is wide open, and you see just the pair you're looking for. The shoes sparkle in multiple colors, with touches of gold and a rhinestone-studded heel.

You try them on. Perfect fit. You'll get them back in the closet before Anabel even notices. You spin in front of the mirror. The glittering lights illuminate your face. You hardly recognize yourself. At the dance, no one else seems to recognize you, either. A new dress, a new hairdo, a little makeup, and suddenly you're transformed from boring old Cinderella to Wowzarella!

You spend most of the night dancing with a handsome boy. Time flies, and when you look up at the clock, you see it's almost midnight. "I have to go," you tell him.

"Just one more song!" he pleads.

You pause to consider. What are the chances the wires will fry at exactly midnight? A few minutes might not hurt anything.

TO DANCE ONE MORE SONG, TURN TO PAGE 40.

TO RETURN THE DRESS TO THE OLD WOMAN, TURN TO PAGE 42.

"My name is Birdie," the girl tells you. Her face rings a bell. You realize she is the girl who works at Princess Patterns, the fabric store in the mall. Maybe she really can help you!

Birdie nods at your ruined dress. "I like your taste. That's a great dress!" she says.

"Was," you mutter. "It's ruined now."

Birdie examines the dress. "Nah. We can do a little ripping here, a little patching there, and maybe add some chenille panels and a starched layer underneath, which will really give the skirt some bounce!"

32

You stare at her as she talks, hardly believing your ears. Here's a girl who loves design as much as you! You go to Birdie's house and get to work on your dress. When it's finished, it's even better than before. "Let's go to the dance!" Birdie says.

When you and Birdie walk into the dance, everyone turns to stare at your gorgeous dresses. "Wow!" you hear someone exclaim.

"Who's that?" another voice asks.

You lead the way to the dance floor, and the crowd parts to let you pass. You feel like a princess in a fairy tale come true. Best of all, you've made a new friend. You and Birdie dance the night away.

THE END

TO FOLLOW ANOTHER PATH, TURN TO PAGE 9.

You walk toward the handsome boy. You smile at him, but he bursts into howling laughter. "You have the ugliest car I've ever seen!" he gasps. "And your clothes are ugly too!"

You are shocked at his rudeness. You realize he's not very handsome at all, not with an attitude like that. Just then, you turn to see Anabel gliding toward you both in a shimmering, golden dress. She waves at the boy and they walk off toward the dance together. You decide they deserve each other.

You walk back over to Rusty and pop the hood. The first thing you should do is check the oil. You pull out the dipstick and look around for something to wipe it off with. Just as you are about to wipe it on your skirt, an arm juts in front of you.

"Use my sleeve," a guy's voice says. Then his head appears around the popped hood. He grabs the stick, wipes it on his sleeve, and checks the oil.

"Oil's fine," he says. He leans under the hood and fiddles with some wires. "Looks like you overheated. I've got some coolant that should do the trick." He smiles at you and you smile back.

He gets Rusty going again and offers to follow you to the dance in his car, just in case anything else goes wrong.

When the two of you arrive at school, you hear a song blaring from the gymnasium.

35

TURN THE PAGE.

"This is my favorite Prince song!" you say, regretting your words immediately. You hope he doesn't think your taste in music is as outdated as your dress.

36

But the boy flashes you a wide grin. "You like Prince?" he asks. "I do too. Let's dance right here!"

THE END

TO FOLLOW ANOTHER PATH, TURN TO PAGE 9.

You buy the car from Diane, and she skips away with your cash in hand. You have no money left to buy a dress, so you decide not to go to the dance. The main reason you wanted to go anyway was a chance to dress up and wear something beautiful instead of your Pizza Palace clothes for a change. "Oh well," you sigh. "I'll just take on an extra shift at the Pizza Palace tonight and start saving money again."

You drive to work in your new orange car. When you walk into the Pizza Palace, you are greeted by one of your coworkers, a friendly guy named Princeton. "Nice car!" he says. You blush, not sure if he's teasing you.

"Why aren't you at the school dance?" you ask him.

TURN THE PAGE.

"I hate dressing up," Princeton says, shrugging.

"I love to dress up!" you tell him, laughing.

Princeton grins. "I should introduce you to my aunt. She loves to dress up too. In fact, she has her own clothing line. Her name's Vivian Marshall."

The pizza pan you are holding clatters to the floor. "She's my favorite!" you gasp.

"Well, you're in luck. She's in town visiting, and she's going to stop in tonight for a pizza."

You are so excited you can hardly concentrate on work. When Vivian Marshall finally comes in, Princeton introduces you. You are nervous, but she's so nice and puts you at ease. You tell her about your interest in fashion design.

"I skipped the dance tonight because I had nothing to wear," you admit.

She nods, understanding. "Tell you what," she says. "I'll visit again before your next school dance, and I'll bring you one of my designs to wear." She pauses, and you stare at her, your mouth handing open. You can hardly believe your ears. "But there's a catch," she continues.

"Anything!" you say.

She jerks her head toward Princeton. "You have to drag my nephew to the dance too."

You and Princeton glance at each other, blushing. "I can do that!" you agree.

39

THE END

TO FOLLOW ANOTHER PATH, TURN TO PAGE 9.

But one more song turns into two, then three. You don't hear the clock strike midnight. You just keep dancing. The dress still shimmers and pops with light. Surely you have a few more minutes.

But before you know it, it's 12:30. You stop dancing and look down at your skirt. It's dead and dark. You give a little shake. Nothing. Not a single spark of light.

"I have to go!" you tell the boy and rush out the door.

You change into your old dress and hurry outside to hand the dress to the old woman. She shakes her head sadly and hands you a bill for the ruined dress. Your eyes pop at the price. You'll have to work extra hours to pay for this. Dejected, you go home.

The next day the boy you danced with comes into the Pizza Palace during your shift. "I was hoping you'd be working," he says.

"How did you find me?" you ask.

"This fell out of your purse when you ran away." He holds up your Pizza Palace name tag. You had been wondering where that was. "Why did you leave so fast last night?" he asks.

You explain to him about the dress. "Now I have to pick up more shifts to pay for it," you sigh, looking down at your Pizza Palace uniform.

"I work at the shoe store across the street. I think I'll be coming over for a lot of pizza breaks," he says with a smile.

41

THE END

TO FOLLOW ANOTHER PATH, TURN TO PAGE 9.

You run as fast as you can from the gymnasium. "Wait!" the boy calls after you. "What's your name?"

You don't want to tell him you are Cinderella, the girl everyone makes fun of. He might not like you anymore. You want him to remember you as a beautiful girl in a shimmering, electric dress. You keep running. You throw on your old clothes, return the designer dress to the old woman, and go home, relieved the boy never discovered your true identity.

When you sneak into Anabel's closet to return her shoes, you realize you must've dropped one. "I'll find it tomorrow," you tell yourself. "She'll never miss it."

The next morning you hear a knock on the front door. You creep to the top of the stairs and see Anabel talking to the boy from the dance. He's holding your lost shoe! Anabel is holding the match.

"We danced all night, and you never told me your name," the boy says.

"It's Anabel," she says. You want to gag.

The two link arms and walk down the sidewalk. You shake your head in disgust. If this guy is clueless enough to mistake Anabel for you, then you're better off without him. You sigh, go back to your room, and start sketching a dress idea for the next school dance.

43

THE END

TO FOLLOW ANOTHER PATH, TURN TO PAGE 9.

At home you fast-forward to the end of the *Real Livin' with Vivian* episode. "If none of these tips work," Vivian is saying, "make the stains look like they're supposed to be there. And you're in luck, because tattered garments are all the rage this season."

You follow her advice, adding ink splotches and bleached elements to create a funky pattern alongside the grease stains. Then you cut the skirt to create a shabby look. You pair the dress with some tall studded boots and twist a few tiny braids and silver ribbons into your hair. Then you stand before the mirror. Not bad, you think.

When you get to the dance, you don't wait around for anyone to ask you to dance. Instead you march to the dance floor alone, feeling confident. A few classmates join you.

Suddenly the music stops and a girl steps onto the stage. You recognize her as the girl you saw in the mall parking lot today. "My name is Birdie," she says. "I'm the president of the school's design club called 'Passion for Fashion.' Tonight we are giving out fashion prizes. First we are giving away the prize for Best Dress."

A hush falls over the crowd. You are about to sneak over to the punch bowl when, to your surprise, she says, "The prize goes to … Cinderella!"

You walk to the stage in disbelief, the crowd clapping around you—except for Anabel and Diane, who glower as you pass. "Congratulations!" Birdie says. She hands you your trophy—a sparkling glass slipper. There is also a gift card for Shoes Royale, Anabel's favorite store. **45**

You smile and take a bow.

THE END

TO FOLLOW ANOTHER PATH, TURN TO PAGE 9.

CHAPTER 3

THE PAUPER AND THE PRINCESS

You are a young man living in Kingdom Faraway, a land with rolling hills and green meadows. In the distance a sparkling castle reaches toward the clouds. The land is beautiful, but your life is one of misery. After your father died, your stepmother ran off with a lord from another kingdom, but not before she fired all the servants.

Now your stepbrothers treat you as their servant-boy. They kicked you out of the family manor and make you live in the rundown servants' cottage.

All day long they order you around. You cook, chop wood, and clean the fireplace while your stepbrothers do nothing but argue about which of them is stronger and compete in ridiculous strength contests.

You hate all the chores. But the manor is your family home, and it must be cared for. Even though the house is small and in disrepair, it is still grand. Your tiny cottage, though, has nothing but four walls, a bed, and a tiny stove. You hate it. You spend your free time sketching architectural designs on your dirt floor.

48

Whenever you are able to slip away, you go to the meadow. There you lie on your back with a view of the royal castle, imagining its curving staircases and stately ballrooms. You long to build or even live in such a castle someday, but you're pretty certain this is as close as you'll ever get.

One day you return home from the meadow to find your stepbrother Wilbur waving a piece of parchment and looking excited.

"The king is throwing a royal ball!" he says. "And we've been invited!"

Your heart lurches. At last, a chance to see the castle!

But Morris, your other stepbrother, can see what you're thinking and laughs. "Not you, silly," he says. "The invitation is addressed to the 'Sons of Lady M.' It says nothing about Asher the servant-boy."

"The ball is for the king's daughter, Princess Charming," Wilbur continues. "Wait 'til she sees my biceps!"

TURN THE PAGE.

Princess Charming is the king's only daughter. He keeps her very protected, and few have ever laid eyes on her. All that's known is that she wears a ruby crown.

On the day of the ball, you are stuck cleaning the fireplace. You would much rather be going to the castle and studying its fireplaces.

As you are brushing the ashes off your clothes, Wilbur comes into the room. "Hey, Cinderfella," he taunts, seeing the ash on your clothes. "My suit needs something for the lapel. Go find me a firebird feather. And don't take all day!"

You love birds and would actually like to see a firebird. But you also are tired of taking orders.

TO FIND A FIREBIRD FEATHER, GO TO PAGE 51.

TO REFUSE, TURN TO PAGE 53.

You set off for the forest. You veer off the worn path and plunge into the dense, overgrown thicket. After a long search, a bright red feather finally catches your eye. Above, you see the quiet firebird quickly flit away. You follow the bird, amazed at its beauty, momentarily forgetting your errand. When you lose sight of the bird, you turn to head back. But you've gone so deep into the forest you don't know which way to go. You wander through the woods, uncertain. You're lost.

At last you come upon a large clearing. Ahead you see a path and a small bridge. Realization hits you: You are on the castle grounds! And a carriage is coming. You have to hide. You can't be caught trespassing.

TURN THE PAGE.

You duck behind a rosebush and watch as the carriage lumbers along the path. You see a heavy curtain being pulled from the window, and then a head pokes out. You glimpse long raven locks and a ruby crown. It's Princess Charming! You gaze at her, stunned. You've never seen such beauty before.

The carriage lurches over the road and bounces over a large rock. Items spill from the back, but the carriage keeps going.

You see something glittering on the road. It's the princess' glass slipper. You should return it to the princess—and win her favor! But you are afraid of being questioned about trespassing on the castle grounds. Besides, the slipper might make a good souvenir.

TO CHASE AFTER THE CARRIAGE AND RETURN THE SLIPPER, TURN TO PAGE 56.

TO KEEP THE SLIPPER AS A SOUVENIR, TURN TO PAGE 57.

"I'm done taking orders from you," you tell
Wilbur. You are out the door before he can say
a word, heading for the meadow. You want to
find the unusual hazel tree near there that you
recently discovered. Its wood would make an
excellent chair for your cottage. But when you
reach the hazel tree, you see that it's no longer a
tall, splendid tree. Instead it's been split in half by
lightning. You groan. You can't possibly make a
solid chair out of what's left.

Small white birds flutter above the tree,
singing loudly. You have an idea. You could build
a magnificent birdhouse from the dead tree—a
miniature castle. But maybe you should keep
searching for a solid tree to build a chair with.
You are getting tired of eating your cold supper
on the dirt floor.

53

TO BUILD THE BIRDHOUSE, TURN TO PAGE 54.

TO CONTINUE SEARCHING, TURN TO PAGE 70.

In the dirt you sketch out your design for the
birdhouse, complete with turrets, towers, and

winding staircases, just for fun. You gather up
pieces of wood and begin building. You don't care
anymore about missing the ball.

When you're finally finished, you stand back
to inspect your work. The white birds zoom in
and out of the bird castle. They are pleased, and
so are you.

At the sound of hooves, you turn to see a lovely young woman astride a white horse. The sun glints off her ruby crown. Princess Charming!

She leaps from her horse and gazes at your birdhouse. "Did you build this?" she asks.

You nod, and she exclaims, "I would like one of my own! I love birds."

You agree, and with the rest of the hazel wood, you construct a second beautiful birdhouse. When it's finished, you deliver it to the castle. The king himself greets you. When he sees your work, he admires it too. He asks if you'd like to help design a new wing for the castle. "Absolutely!" you say, already imagining spiraling staircases, fine crown molding, and no more cleaning out fireplaces.

55

THE END

TO FOLLOW ANOTHER PATH, TURN TO PAGE 9.

You slide the slipper into your pocket and run after the carriage yelling, "Stop!"

The carriage slows, and the guards turn to you. "Halt!" one yells.

You reach into your pocket to draw out the glass slipper. As you do so, the guards rush toward you, swords drawn. They think you're reaching for a weapon! "I just want to speak with the princess," you say, putting your hands up.

The princess leans out of the carriage. "He must earn his right to speak with me," she challenges.

56   One of the guards grins. "I love a good fight. A sword fight with me? Or will you run, coward?"

You're more interested in the craftsmanship of swords than fighting with them. But this may be your only chance to talk to the princess.

TO RUN AWAY, GO TO PAGE 57.

TO AGREE TO A FIGHT, TURN TO PAGE 58.

You run for home, feeling like a coward.

As Wilbur and Morris get ready for the ball, you finish your chores and gaze out the window. You dream about life in another kingdom, away from your stepbrothers' demands. With your building skills, surely you'll find work. You decide it's time to take action. You throw your few belongings—and the glass slipper—into a knapsack. But before you can get away, Wilbur and Morris emerge from the manor, ready for the ball. "Take us to the castle!" Morris orders.

You're irritated. Now that you've decided to leave, you're anxious to go right away. However, if you take them to the ball, you might have a chance to see the castle … and Princess Charming again.

57

TO TAKE YOUR STEPBROTHERS TO THE BALL, TURN TO PAGE 60.

TO REFUSE AND VENTURE OUT ON YOUR OWN, TURN TO PAGE 74.

"Toss me a sword!" you say, hoping your show of bravery will impress the princess.

One of the guards hands you a sword, and you try not to wince at its weight. Your hands shake as you clutch the hilt and raise the sword in the air. The guards chuckle. Your face burns. You hope the princess can't see your trembling hands.

"My money's on Rolf!" one of the guards says. They all burst into laughter.

Rolf raises his sword, and you take a swing. He smashes his sword against yours. Somehow you evade his jabs, ducking and hopping. You've never been so scared.

Rolf swipes at you, and you dance backward, avoiding the blade until he has you pinned against a giant tree. You can't move.

Rolf shoves you to the ground and when you hit, the glass slipper rolls from your pocket. The princess marches over and snatches up the slipper. Glowering at you, she says, "Step aside, Rolf. I'll take care of him."

She raises the slipper and thumps you on the head with it. Ouch! You think a stab of the sword might've hurt less.

You sit up, rubbing your forehead, as the carriage rolls away, . You're pretty sure you've just ruined any chance you ever had of seeing the castle.

59

THE END

TO FOLLOW ANOTHER PATH, TURN TO PAGE 9.

Your stepbrothers climb into the run-down carriage. As you take them toward the castle, you grit your teeth and try to tune out their argument about which of them has the stronger jawline.

You park the carriage at the castle gates, and your stepbrothers strut up the steps in their outdated but still regal suits.

You stand outside the carriage, wondering if you could just peek inside the castle. You look down at your ragged, dirty clothes. There's no way the royal guards will let you even come close to the castle doors.

But you do have the princess' glass slipper in your pocket. You could tell the guards you just want to return it.

As you are debating what to do, you notice an
old man near the castle gates, watching you. He
has a long, straggly beard, a tall pointed hat, and
a mysterious glint in his eyes. You shiver. "Asher!"
he calls to you. How does he know your name?
He waves at you to come closer.

TO IGNORE THE MAN AND SNEAK INTO THE BALL,
TURN TO PAGE 62.

TO TALK TO THE OLD MAN, TURN TO PAGE 64.

You march confidently up the castle stairs to the main entrance. You tell the guard you are a shoe repairman, here to return the princess' glass slipper, which you pull out of your pocket.

To your surprise, he lets you pass. You wander through the maze of hallways to the ballroom where chandeliers flicker and the orchestra plays. You admire the grand columns and Gothic archways. Suddenly a castle guard steps in front of you, looking you up and down. "No peasants allowed," he booms.

Over the guard's shoulder, you see Princess Charming making her grand entrance. The ruby crown on her head sparkles in the candlelight. As she steps across the dance floor, you notice she's wearing only one glass slipper.

Now is your chance! "Princess Charming!" you call, waving the slipper in the air.

The princess whirls to look at you. The orchestra stops playing, and silence falls on the crowd. You can hear your heart hammering. The princess' eyes travel to the slipper in your hand. You expect her to smile gratefully, but instead shock and anger cross her face. "Thief!" she cries. "To the dungeon with him!"

Royal guards grab your arms roughly.

"Wait!" you say. You cast a final pleading look at your stepbrothers, but they are busy making pigs of themselves at the buffet table.

The guards drag you from the ballroom to the dank, dark dungeon, where you will live out your days as a prisoner. You got your wish to live in the castle, but the dungeon is all you'll see.

63

THE END

TO FOLLOW ANOTHER PATH, TURN TO PAGE 9.

You approach the old man carefully. You're surprised to see him drop into a bow. "Wizard Godfather, at your service," he says. "Your long-suffering patience is being rewarded. For one night you will have all the honor and respect you ever wished for."

He pulls a wand out of his hat and waves it over your head. "What's going on?" you cry. Then you look down and see that you are suddenly wearing a fancy cape and tunic. You look like a nobleman! You can easily get into the ball now.

"Beware," the wizard cautions. "The spell will wear off at midnight."

64

You head toward the castle. Stepping through the doors, you look around. Sparkling chandeliers swing from the ceiling. Curved staircases climb upward. The castle is even more magnificent than you imagined.

Soon the princess makes her grand entrance. The ruby crown on her head sparkles in the candlelight, and you see she's wearing only one glass slipper! Immediately knights and lords approach her, lining up to dance with her. You sigh. It will be a long wait.

Then you notice Morris across the ballroom. He's on the floor clutching his back and writhing in pain. Wilbur is nowhere to be seen.

TO WAIT TO DANCE WITH THE PRINCESS, TURN TO PAGE 66.

TO HELP MORRIS, TURN TO PAGE 68.

65

You decide against approaching Morris. He will just blow your cover. You wait your turn to dance with the princess as she whirls and waltzes with other knights in fancy suits and shining armor. You nervously watch the clock. It's an exquisite timepiece, you can't help but notice. At last, it's your turn.

But just as you offer the princess your arm, the clock chimes midnight. Your fancy clothes fall to pieces around you. You're left standing in your tattered work clothes. While the princess stares at you in horror, the glass slipper slides from your pocket and crashes to the floor, shattering to bits.

The music stops. Everyone turns to stare.

"My glass slipper!" the princess sobs. "You stole it … and now broke it!"

The royal guards grab you. You are put on trial and sentenced to five years of labor, working for the village glassblower.

The work is hot and difficult, but you soon discover you love glassblowing—and you're away from your stepbrothers! You have a gift for designing elaborate glass pieces. You even make a tiny glass slipper that you give the princess as an apology.

To your astonishment, Princess Charming is so taken with the artistry of your glass that she asks you to design her something else: a new castle.

67

THE END

TO FOLLOW ANOTHER PATH, TURN TO PAGE 9.

You rush over to Morris and ask what's wrong.

"My back, you fool! I tried to lift that

sculpture to impress the princess, and something in my back snapped!" You look over to see a large marble statue of a man on a horse, and you wonder which of you is the fool.

As you are helping him to a chair, you feel a tap on your shoulder. You turn to see Princess Charming smiling at you.

She tells you she admires you for helping a "poor witless creature," and she wants to dance with you next.

You whirl her around the dance floor, hoping the song will never end. But when it does, you pull her glass slipper from beneath your vest. "It might be easier to dance with two of these," you tell her. The princess grabs the shoe and you're afraid she might be angry. But she breaks into a smile. "Thank you!" she says as she slides the slipper onto her foot. "Can we dance another?"

You dance all night, and just before midnight you bid the princess farewell. "Please visit me tomorrow," she says. You smile and know that you will visit her the next day and the day after that and the day after that …

69

THE END

TO FOLLOW ANOTHER PATH, TURN TO PAGE 9.

You follow the path through the woods, scanning your surroundings for another hazel tree. As you proceed deeper into the woods, you hear the sound of rushing water. You emerge from the forest to see a waterfall cascading from a high cliff. At the bottom of the waterfall, several people splash and swim. A ruby crown sparkles on one of the girls' heads. It's Princess Charming! Your heart leaps at her beauty.

A shadow passes over you. You look up to see a bright orange dragon flapping across the sky. The dragon lands on the cliff above the waterfall and stares down at the swimmers, nostrils flaring. You are frightened, but no one in the royal group seems to notice the dragon. You gulp. The princess could be in danger!

TO JUMP INTO THE WATER TO WARN THE PRINCESS, GO TO PAGE 71.

TO CONFRONT THE DRAGON, TURN TO PAGE 72.

You jump into the water, yelling as you swim toward the group. As you near them, you look up and see the dragon open its giant mouth and spew orange flames at you. You kick frantically, but there's no escape. Your hair catches fire and you duck under the water to put it out.

Just then someone grabs you and pulls you to shore. "Are you all right?" the princess asks. She shakes her fist at the dragon. "Naughty Pumpkin!" The dragon just shrugs.

"That's my dragon, Pumpkin," she explains. "He was trying to protect me. Would you like an invitation to the ball as an apology?"

71

You nod your singed head. The princess leans down and whispers into your ear, "I'll save the first dance for you."

THE END

TO FOLLOW ANOTHER PATH, TURN TO PAGE 9.

You creep toward the dragon. When he spots you, his fiery eyes blaze. "What do you want?" he growls. With all your might, you charge at him and thrust your knife into his chest. He slumps to the ground, orange blood oozing from his wound.

The princess scrambles out of the pond and up the hill. "What have you done to my dragon?" she screams, running to the beast's side. "Pumpkin, are you okay?"

Pumpkin opens his eyes and glares at you. He closes up his wound with a burst of flame from his nostrils and rises to his feet. He's alive, which is good ... but not for you. You back away. The dragon rears his head, opens his wide mouth, and shoots a wall of flames at you, burning you to a crisp. Cinderfella, after all.

THE END

TO FOLLOW ANOTHER PATH, TURN TO PAGE 9.

"I'm not your servant!" you say. "I won't take you to the ball."

Wilbur gasps, and Morris lets out an angry roar. You run for the woods, and your stepbrothers chase after you. But you weave through the trees and quickly lose them. Dragging all those muscles around makes them slow as molasses. Breathless, you plop down next to a stream, slide the slipper into the water, and take a long drink from its heel.

"Ahem!" says a voice behind you. You turn to see a strange man with a long gray beard, pointed hat, and walking stick hobbling toward you. He huffs and puffs. "You are hard to catch!" he wheezes.

You scramble to your feet, ready to run, but he laughs. "Don't be afraid." He clears his throat again and sings shrilly, "I am your Wizard Godfather!"

You wince at his awful singing voice. Then you register his words. "Wizard Godfather?"

He nods. "I roam kingdoms far and wide, bestowing gifts upon deserving, hardworking lads and ladies. Now, what do you wish for?"

You don't hesitate. "To be rid of my stepbrothers. And to live in my father's manor again. Oh, and to see the royal castle!"

"Easy task!" cries the wizard. He waves the walking stick over his head. "Done."

You blink. "Done?"

"Follow that path to your new destiny." The wizard shuffles off into the woods. You follow the path until you reach a large manor, identical to your **75** family home, minus Wilbur and Morris. An envelope lies inside the door. An invitation to the ball. This time, it has your name on it.

THE END

TO FOLLOW ANOTHER PATH, TURN TO PAGE 9.

CHAPTER 4

DRELLA IN SPACE

"My ship is broken down again!" your stepsister Quin complains. "Fix it!"

Sighing, you step out the door of your spacehut to take a look. You know just how to fix it, and soon the engine purrs to life. You wonder how she manages to break her spaceship all the time. She has one of the best ships on the planet of Quog. Your other stepsister, Jilli, had one too, until she crashed it playing bumper ships with her friends. Bumper ships! You shake your head in disgust. Even though the girls are so careless, your stepmother keeps buying them new ships. Jilli's will be delivered any day now.

77

After you fix Quin's ship, you look at the sky, watching spaceships whiz and whirl. You long to join them, but you have too much work to do at your job as spaceship mechanic. Maybe later you can buzz around in your old black-and-orange spaceship, which you've fondly named Jacko Lantern. You are one of the best—and youngest—pilots on the planet. Your dream is to become a royal pilot on the planet of Fara. But you don't know how you'll ever achieve your dream.

Quin steps out the door of her spacehut. **78** "Have you fixed it yet?" she demands.

"Yes," you tell her. "You really need to learn not to grind the gears—"

"Whatever," she interrupts, pushing past you and climbing into the ship. She grinds the gears as she starts the engine. You sigh.

Just then a hologram appears. "Attention, all in the Kingdom of Zyralla!" the king booms. "The prince has need of a new pilot. A competition to select one will be held tomorrow on Fara."

Tomorrow! Your mind races. This is a chance to achieve your dream! But first you have a lot of work to do on Jacko to get it ready.

Quin hops out of her spaceship. "Did you hear that? I'm going to audition!" You glare at her. She doesn't want to be a royal pilot. She just wants to cozy up to the prince. You head toward Jacko.

"Wait! You have to help get my ship ready!"

79

If you don't help her, your stepmother might take away your flying privileges. But you don't have time to help Quin and fix Jacko.

TO HELP QUIN, TURN TO PAGE 80.

TO FIX JACKO, TURN TO PAGE 83.

You work all night, fixing up Quin's spaceship until it shines and glides. She doesn't even thank you before speeding off toward Fara the next morning. You take another look at Jacko and sigh. You'll never make it to the competition now.

Another hologram appears in front of you. This time it's your godmother, Lyra. She lives two planets away but often pops up to check on you.

She peers through the hologram. "Is that you, Drella? Did you hear the king's announcement, dear? Of course you did. Well, I heard you helped Quin, and that's wonderful, though I can't imagine what she's thinking. That girl can't even take off without ruining the transmission. Anyway, dear, I have a present for you. Just a little magic trick I picked up."

"Magic trick?" you ask, skeptical.

"Magic, you know, like abracadabra!" she says.
She closes her eyes to think. "Okay. Arba!" she
chants. "Dacar! Ba!"

Lyra opens her eyes. "Ta-da!" she sings.

"Nothing happened," you tell her, trying not
to giggle.

"Turn around, dear."

TURN THE PAGE.

You turn to see that Jacko is gone. A fabulous new spaceship is in its place. "Wow!" you whisper. It's a Carriage5000, the fastest ship ever invented! You run your hand across the spaceship's sleek side.

"Good luck at the competition," Lyra says. "But beware. The spell will wear off at midnight and Jacko will be back. Oh, and here's the spare key. Don't lose it!" She tosses a sparkling glass key through the hologram and disappears.

You climb into the Carriage5000 and zoom off. You've never flown outside Quog's orbit. You're busy enjoying all the bells and whistles of the new ship when you realize you might be lost. Up ahead, you see the lights of another spaceship. You could stop and ask the pilot for directions, or keep going on your own.

TO ASK FOR DIRECTIONS, TURN TO PAGE 88.

TO KEEP GOING, TURN TO PAGE 92.

You spend all night replacing Jacko's parts, fixing broken springs, and checking gauges. Meanwhile Quin speeds away toward Fara in a huff, and Jilli jeers at you from the window of her spacehut. Luckily your stepmother is on an intergalactic shopping trip, so your stepsisters can't to tattle on you for not helping Quin.

At last you are finished. You leap into Jacko, start the engine, and power into space. After a while you look down at the gauges to make sure everything is working correctly. Fara is farther than you thought and you're running low on fuel.

Just ahead you see a glowing ball of light. It grows larger as you rocket toward it. You slow to a stop and see that it's not a planet but millions of tiny space bugs caught in the gravitational pull of a nearby moon.

83

TURN THE PAGE.

"Please help us!" There's no sound in space, so you're surprised to hear their cry. You realize they're speaking to you telepathically! They must be very

evolved space bugs to have developed that skill. You know you'll waste fuel by stopping to help, but if you don't, they'll be caught there forever.

TO HELP THE SPACE BUGS, GO TO PAGE 85.

TO CONTINUE ON, TURN TO PAGE 87.

You can't just leave them there. You hop out of the ship in your space suit. You decide to give the telepathic communication a try. "How can I help?" you think as hard as you can. To your surprise, they actually respond.

They tell you that if you tug just one of them out, it will be enough to break the gravity and release all of them. You pull one bug, and the cloud breaks apart. You are blinded by the bright lights of the bugs as they surround you. Blinking, you see that as a group they have transformed into a shimmering fairy.

85

"Since you helped us, we'll help you," the fairy says. She waves a wand and your Jacko changes to a Carriage5000, the fastest and sleekest ship ever invented! She hands you a sparkling glass key.

TURN THE PAGE.

"Don't lose this spare key," she says. "And beware, the spell breaks at midnight."

You thank her and fly away, excited to actually be flying a Carriage5000! You're so amazed by the beautiful ship that you almost forget about the competition. And then you realize you might be lost. Up ahead, you see a fancy spaceship. You send a radio signal asking for directions.

"I can plug the route into your system," the pilot answers in a muffled voice. "But first I need to board your ship."

TO ALLOW THE PILOT TO BOARD, TURN TO PAGE 89.

TO KEEP GOING, TURN TO PAGE 105.

As you continue toward Fara, you see a
spaceship up ahead, not moving. It looks like the
pilot is in trouble. When you get closer to the
spaceship, you realize it's Quin. You could stop
to help, but you'll waste time.

TO HELP QUIN, TURN TO PAGE 98.

TO KEEP GOING, TURN TO PAGE 105.

As you approach the spaceship, you see it's a Fantasy Cruiser, one of the newest ships on the market. You've never seen one in person before. You hover next to it and send a radio signal. "Do you know the way to Fara?" you ask.

The pilot's muffled voice responds through your speakers. "I can plug the route into your navigation system," the pilot says. The voice is familiar, but you can't place it. "But I need to board your ship."

You're not sure if you should trust the strange pilot. But you really need to get directions to Fara or you'll miss the contest.

88

TO ALLOW THE PILOT TO BOARD, GO TO PAGE 89.

TO FIND YOUR OWN WAY, TURN TO PAGE 92.

You don't see what choice you have if you want to get to the contest on time. You send a space ladder to the Fantasy, and the pilot crawls across onto your ship. The pilot is wearing a full space suit with a helmet covering the face.

You stand back as the pilot fiddles with your controls. "There you go!" the pilot says in an oddly deep voice, then climbs back across the ladder to the Fantasy and zooms away.

You sit back and let the navigation system take over. You pass planet after planet. You expect to see a lot of traffic heading toward Fara, but strangely you don't see any. You study the galaxy maps again. Your final destination is Fara, but you discover you are taking the long way around.

89

TURN THE PAGE.

Your radio crackles. "Enjoying the view?" says a deep voice on the other end. It's the strange Fantasy pilot. Then the voice breaks into a familiar high-pitched laugh. Jilli! You realize she was the strange pilot all along. In her brand-new Fantasy Cruiser.

"You sabotaged me!" you cry, but the radio has clicked off.

You fiddle with the controls. "Navigation locked," an automated voice tells you.

Groaning, you realize you might not make it to Fara in time for the competition. All you can do is wait.

At last you see Fara. As you come closer, sparkling palaces appear. Fara is beautiful! The competition is already under way. You quickly dock the ship and find the nearest royal official. "I'd like to add my name to the competition," you tell him.

"You're awfully late," he says, tapping on his device. "I'll add your name, but there might not be time for you."

You see Quin waiting her turn to compete. You watch the others fly the course. They're not good at all. You can win this for sure. But then again, even Quin could beat these pilots—as long as she doesn't kill her engine. She just might win if you don't get a chance to fly.

Jilli's trick on you has sparked an idea. You could sabotage Quin's controls. That way, Quin definitely won't win. But you're not sure you want to stoop to your stepsisters' level.

91

TO SABOTAGE QUIN, TURN TO PAGE 100.

TO WAIT YOUR TURN, TURN TO PAGE 101.

You zoom into the darkness, unsure of where you are going. The space outside Quog is so vast! As you fly in what you hope is the right direction, you hear a strange noise in the engine. You set your ship to autopilot and go to the engine room to investigate.

There you find two gigantic flying space-rats stuck in the engine. You've never seen such big, ugly rats before. Yuck! They squeak at you as you pull them from the engine and open the hatch, hoping they'll fly away into space. But their squeaky chatter only gets louder and faster. They clearly don't want to leave. Are they trying to tell you something?

TO SHOO THE RATS OUT THE HATCH, GO TO PAGE 93.

TO LET THE RATS STAY, TURN TO PAGE 95.

You grab a wrench and nudge the rats out
the hatch. Whew! You breathe a sigh of relief
to have those icky rats off your ship. You watch
them flutter through space. Then all of a sudden
you remember. They weren't rats at all. They
were Coachmen—high-tech navigational devices
that could have helped you get to Fara quickly.
Big mistake.

TURN THE PAGE.

Now you are completely lost. You try to radio for help, but you can't pick up a signal. You fly for hours, getting more hopelessly lost. You've missed the competition and you're still flying when midnight strikes. Your Carriage5000 shudders violently, turns back into Jacko, and promptly breaks down. This time it seems to be for good, because after hours of trying, you can't get it going again. Maybe you're not such an ace mechanic after all. You sit and wait, hoping someone in the galaxy will find you. But you're not holding your breath.

94

THE END

TO FOLLOW ANOTHER PATH, TURN TO PAGE 9.

You close the hatch in frustration. The rats' squeaking just gets louder. Finally you realize that they are chirping in a familiar rhythm. Where have you heard it before? It's a song from a commercial for Coachmen, which are navigational devices for spaceships! They aren't rats at all! Your godmother didn't mention that this ship came equipped with them. What luck!

You gather the Coachmen and open a hatch with a compass painted on it. There you discover a digital rat maze on a tabletop screen. One rat jumps onto the screen. The other begins punching buttons on nearby controls, causing a digital image of Fara to appear on the maze. The running rat whirs into action, working its way through the complex maze toward Fara. You hear the spaceship's engine kick into gear. You reach your destination in no time.

TURN THE PAGE.

95

At last it is your turn to fly. You zoom through the air, showing off your piloting skills as you dodge obstacles. Then you decide to add a little spice with your special trick, a quadruple backward loop. You land to the roar of applause.

After all the contestants have flown, the king collects everyone's keys. "I will announce the winner by displaying the pilot's key," he says. "But first, we party!"

You glance at the hovering space-clock above the contest grounds. It's nearly midnight. You should return to Quog before your Carriage5000 turns back into Jacko. But you can't leave before they announce the winner. It's possible you've won, and you don't want them to give the prize to someone else if you're not there.

TO STAY FOR THE PARTY, GO TO PAGE 97.

TO GO HOME, TURN TO PAGE 104.

You have a great time at the party. It's past midnight when the award ceremony begins. Your Carriage5000 has turned back into Jacko. The king holds up a glass key—yours. You've won! He asks that the winner drive his or her spaceship forward. But when you approach with Jacko, he frowns. "That's not the right spaceship," the king says, looking down at the glass key in his hand.

"But ... " you say, desperately. "I can prove I was the winning pilot. I have a key to match!" You reach into your pocket and hand him the spare.

The king holds up both keys, still frowning. You hold your breath. Finally he shrugs and nods. "Well, then, congratulations! But please, remove that thing from our sight. You'll be flying only top-notch ships from now on."

97

THE END

TO FOLLOW ANOTHER PATH, TURN TO PAGE 9.

Quin looks over at you irritably as you glide up next to her. "Fix my ship. And make it snappy!"

You fix the engine quickly, as usual. "That should do it," you tell her, and Quin zooms off. You crawl back into Jacko and head to Fara, just in time for the competition. You gaze around at the marvelous ships that seem as fast as lightning and stealthy as cats. "There's no way I can win with Jacko," you think miserably.

And you don't. Instead, to your surprise and disappointment, Quin wins. You're even more surprised when the king approaches you after the contest and asks if you'll be the prince's mechanic. "Anyone who can keep that hunk of junk flying has got to be an ace mechanic," he says, gesturing toward Jacko.

So you don't get to be a royal pilot, but you do get to live on Fara. The handsome prince is interested in your mechanical skills and asks for lessons. It is Quin's turn to be shocked when the prince asks you to marry him. Quin is horrified to discover that she now must take orders from you. The first and last order to her: Return to Quog. Once that's settled, you hop into the cockpit of the prince's ship and the two of you jet off into the galaxy together.

99

THE END

You log into the controls and lock the navigation so Quin's ship can only fly straight—no turns or loops. She takes off amidst a round of applause, but the applause dies out as she tries to turn and fails. You're not proud as you see Quin failing, but you convince yourself that she deserves it.

Quin lands and stomps away. Now it is your turn. But just as you launch your ship into the air, midnight strikes. Drat! The Carriage5000 begins to vibrate. With a loud pop, you're sitting back in the cockpit of Jacko. And the engine won't start. It serves you right, you think, as Jacko drops from the sky and rumbles to a stop just inches from the king. "Sorry?" you say weakly.

100

"Your flying license is hereby revoked!" the king thunders.

THE END

TO FOLLOW ANOTHER PATH, TURN TO PAGE 9.

You wait your turn and watch Quin perform. You don't think she'll do very well—after all, you know what a horrible pilot she is. But she surprises you by whizzing through the obstacle course with ease. Then, just before she goes for the landing, she launches into a backward quadruple loop.

Your mouth drops. The backward quadruple is your very own special trick. She must've watched you do it back on Quog, and now she has copied you!

When it's your turn to fly, you're not sure what to do. You could perform the special trick yourself, but then you will look like the copycat. You could try a new trick instead, but you're not sure you can pull it off.

TO PERFORM THE SAME TRICK, TURN TO PAGE 102.

TO PERFORM A NEW TRICK, TURN TO PAGE 103.

You perform the same trick, and to your relief, you do it much better than Quin. The king collects everyone's keys and says he will declare the winner by holding up the winner's key. While the king and prince deliberate, you pace around your ship. You want this so much! To escape your life, to achieve your dream!

Finally the king is ready. With much fanfare, he holds up your glass key and announces that the owner of the matching key is the winner! You squeal with excitement and go to collect your prize. But Quin has gotten there first. She is holding your spare key! You reach into your pocket and realize it's gone. How on earth did she get it?

"You're not the only one with a fairy godmother," she whispers to you with an evil grin.

THE END

TO FOLLOW ANOTHER PATH, TURN TO PAGE 9.

You perform a new trick—a triple left loop-de-loop—and although it goes okay, Quin's quadruple was better. You try not to cry as the king declares Quin the winner.

But as you turn away, dejected, someone taps you on the shoulder. "Miss?" a man in royal attire says. He introduces himself as Prince Charmels from the planet Schmeck. "I couldn't help but be glad that you didn't win this contest … because I was really hoping that you'd come fly for me," he says. He tells you he wants you to be a pilot on his royal space fleet. Then he shows you his brand-new Fortress spacecraft.

"When can I start?" you ask, overjoyed.

THE END

TO FOLLOW ANOTHER PATH, TURN TO PAGE 9.

You make it home safe and sound before midnight. In the morning the king sends a hologram announcement to the kingdom. "The winning pilot left before the award ceremony," he says. "So the runner-up is our new winner!" He steps aside, and Quin appears next to him, smiling widely. "Quin of Planet Quog!"

Next to you, Jilli claps with glee. You clench your jaw and swallow your tears. At least you won't have to service Quin's spaceship anymore. And you'll have one less stepsister to deal with.

104

THE END

TO FOLLOW ANOTHER PATH, TURN TO PAGE 9.

After a few wrong turns, you finally see the bright lights of Fara. You are almost there! But just as your ship's clock buzzes midnight, you hear a chugging sound. Out of gas! You're going to have to make a crash landing, right in the middle of the competition grounds. You steel yourself for the impact. Jacko bounces once, then twice, then tumbles to a stop. You crawl out of the wrecked spaceship. The king and the prince are staring at you. When they see you're not hurt, they burst into laughter. The stunned crowd starts laughing too. "Was that your audition?" the king gasps between chuckles. "You're dismissed!"

105

You'll never be a royal pilot. You take no comfort in knowing that Quin won't either, because it means you'll be back to fixing her ship.

THE END

TO FOLLOW ANOTHER PATH, TURN TO PAGE 9.

CHAPTER 5

CINDERELLA AROUND THE WORLD

From ancient times to the present, the rags-to-riches story of Cinderella has captured imaginations, both young and old. A poor girl living with evil stepsisters overcomes her plight, winning the hearts of many.

One of the earliest Cinderella tales was told in the first century BC. In the tale a Greek girl named Rhodopis is sold into slavery in Egypt. When the Pharaoh holds a ball, the other slave girls leave Rhodopis behind. The god Horus, disguised as a falcon, swoops down, steals one of her shoes, and drops it in the Pharaoh's lap.

The Pharaoh believes it is a sign from the gods and vows to marry the girl who fits the shoe. He travels along the Nile River until he finds Rhodopis. The shoe fits her perfectly, and she becomes the Pharaoh's wife.

In a story from China, young Yeh-Shen is beautiful and kind, but her stepmother and stepsister hate her, forcing her to work constantly. Yeh-Shen's only friend is a large fish with big golden eyes. One day, out of spite, the stepmother and stepsister kill the fish and eat it. Saddened, Yeh-Shen keeps the fish bones. When the spring festival approaches, she wishes upon the bones for something to wear, and the fish's spirit gives her a beautiful dress and golden slippers. After the festival she runs away so quickly that one of her slippers falls off. A king finds it. When Yeh-Shen comes forward to retrieve the slipper, the king asks her to be his wife.

In the Brothers Grimm tale from Germany, a hazel tree grows over Cinderella's mother's grave, and magical white birds sew her a ball gown.

Perhaps the most well-known version of Cinderella was written down by French folklorist, Charles Perrault. In his tale Cinderella's stepmother and stepsisters make her work all day. The prince holds a ball, but Cinderella cannot go because she is just a maid. Then Cinderella's Fairy Godmother casts a spell, turning a pumpkin into a carriage, mice into horses, a rat into a coachman, and Cinderella's rags into a beautiful gown. At midnight the spell will wear off.

The prince is entranced by Cinderella, but she runs away before midnight, leaving behind a glass slipper. The prince vows to marry the girl with the slipper and goes from house to house to find her. The stepsisters try to force the slipper on, but it fits only Cinderella. She marries the prince.

Researchers have traced hundreds of Cinderella versions to many cultures and countries around the world. The versions are different, but each involves an ill-treated youth who rises from the ashes to achieve a dream.

The Cinderella fairy tale has spawned many works of art throughout the ages. Poems, paintings, and plays tell Cinderella's story. Walt Disney released the animated musical film *Cinderella* in 1950. It has become a beloved classic.

The story of Cinderella will continue to be told far and wide, from culture to culture, from book to screen, and from parent to child. In this way, Cinderella and her story will live ever after.

CRITICAL THINKING
USING THE COMMON CORE

On page 107 the author describes *Cinderella* as a "rags-to-riches" story. What does she mean by that? Can you think of other "rags-to-riches" stories? (Craft and Structure)

This book tells three stories, each featuring a different version of the Cinderella character. How might the original story be different if it were told from the stepsisters' or fairy godmother's point of view? (Key Ideas and Details)

Imagine your own Cinderella story. What is the setting? How would the characters and plot be different from the original tale? Can you think of another way you would like the story to end? (Integration of Knowledge and Ideas)

READ MORE

Bradman, Tony. *Cinderella and the Mean Queen.*
North Mankato: Stone Arch Books, 2009.

Comeau, Joey. *Ninja-rella: A Graphic Novel.*
North Mankato: Stone Arch Books, 2015.

Doherty, Berlie. *Classic Fairy Tales: Candlewick Illustrated
Classic.* Somerville, Mass.: Candlewick Press, 2009.

INTERNET SITES

Use FactHound to find Internet sites related to this book.
All of the sites on FactHound have been researched by our staff.

Here's all you do:

Visit *www.facthound.com*

Type in this code: 9781491458549